MEET *FUNKY* NICKY
BY JOANNE VERNEY

IN THE MIDDLE OF HUDSON STREET
WHERE THE SAP TREES GROW STICKY
LIVES A SPUNKY LITTLE GIRL
NAMED *FUNKY* NICKY

NICKY LOVES TO WEAR TOPS WITH POLKA DOTS
AND LEGGINGS WITH STRIPES AT THE SAME TIME
YIPES!!

SHE STANDS A TALL 41 AND ¾ INCHES
FROM HER HEEL TO HER HEAD
HER FAVORITE COLOR IS PURPLE
NOT EMERALD, NOT RED
41 3/4

NICKY LOVES TO BAKE COOKIES
AND PLANT FLOWERS IN A ROW
BUT HER FAVORITE THING TO DO
IS TO SHOOT A BOW!

NICKY LIVES WITH HER MOM
SILLY SALLY YOU SEE
HER DAD KOOKY KENT
AND HER PUPPY BAILEE

SILLY SALLY IS A TEACHER OF MUSIC
WHICH IS JUST FINE WITH NICKY
BUT REACHING HER FROM 9 TO 3
CAN BE KIND OF TRICKY

HER DAD KOOKY KENT
IS UNUSUALLY TALL
WHICH MAKES HIM A
NATURAL AT BASKETBALL

NICKY'S DOG BAILEE
IS QUITE SMALL AND WHITE
TAKE AWAY HER CHEW TOY
AND SHE'LL PUT UP A FIGHT!

NICKY'S BESTIES ARE PHIA AND GEEA
AND JOSEPH AND JUDE
WHO LOVES TO EAT EVERYTHING
EVEN HEALTHY FOOD!!

PHIA IS ALWAYS ACTING AND SINGING
AND WHEN SHE IS NOT
SHE'S SIMPLY SWINGING AND SWINGING

YOU WON'T EVER FIND GEEA
EATING A TORTILLA
BUT YOU MAY FIND HER MUNCHING
AN APPLE WHILE LUNCHING

LET S NOT FORGET JOSEPH
SOME CALL HIM JOE
HE FILLS HIS BELLY WITH BAGELS
AND HAS A WEIRD BIG TOE

NOW HUDSON STREET
MOST SAY IS UNUSUALLY QUIET
HOWEVER ONE VERY ODD DAY
THERE WAS A QUIET RIOT

NICKY'S NEIGHBOR'S CAT JESEE

WAS STUCK IN A TREE

NICKY SHOUTED, "WE'VE GOT TO GET HIM DOWN...

WE'VE GOT TO SET HIM FREE!"

BY NOW THE NEIGHBORS WERE GATHERING
THEY STARTED PLEADING TOO
EVEN OLD MAN TATE
TOSSED UP HIS SHOE!!

TWIN NEIGHBORS BEGAN TO CLIMB THE TREE
THEIR NAMES ARE DREEA & LISS
THEIR FEET ARE SOOO LONG,
THEY ARE REALLY HARD TO MISS.

DOWN THE STREET NEIGHBORS MR MIKE AND MR ADAM
THEY THINK THEY ARE SO SMART
MR MIKE PULLED OUT A MAP
MR ADAM PULLED OUT A CHART

MR. STEAVE (WHO HAS HAIRY EARS)
SAID WITH A FROWN,
"WE MUST RESEARCH, RESEARCH, RESEARCH
HOW TO GET THAT DARN CAT DOWN."
CAT RESCUE

BUT WHY IS JESSEE SO FRIGHTENED?
WHAT COULD BE WRONG?
"I KNOW!" SHOUTED NICKY...
"LET'S SING A SONG!"

AND IN THE NEXT INSTANT
THEY ALL SANG "THREE BLIND MICE"
NOT JUST ONCE OR EVEN TWICE
BUT ACTUALLY THRICE!

BEFORE YOU KNOW IT
JESSEE STARTED TO CLIMB DOWN
EVEN OLD MAN TATE
COULD NOT MUSTER A FROWN.

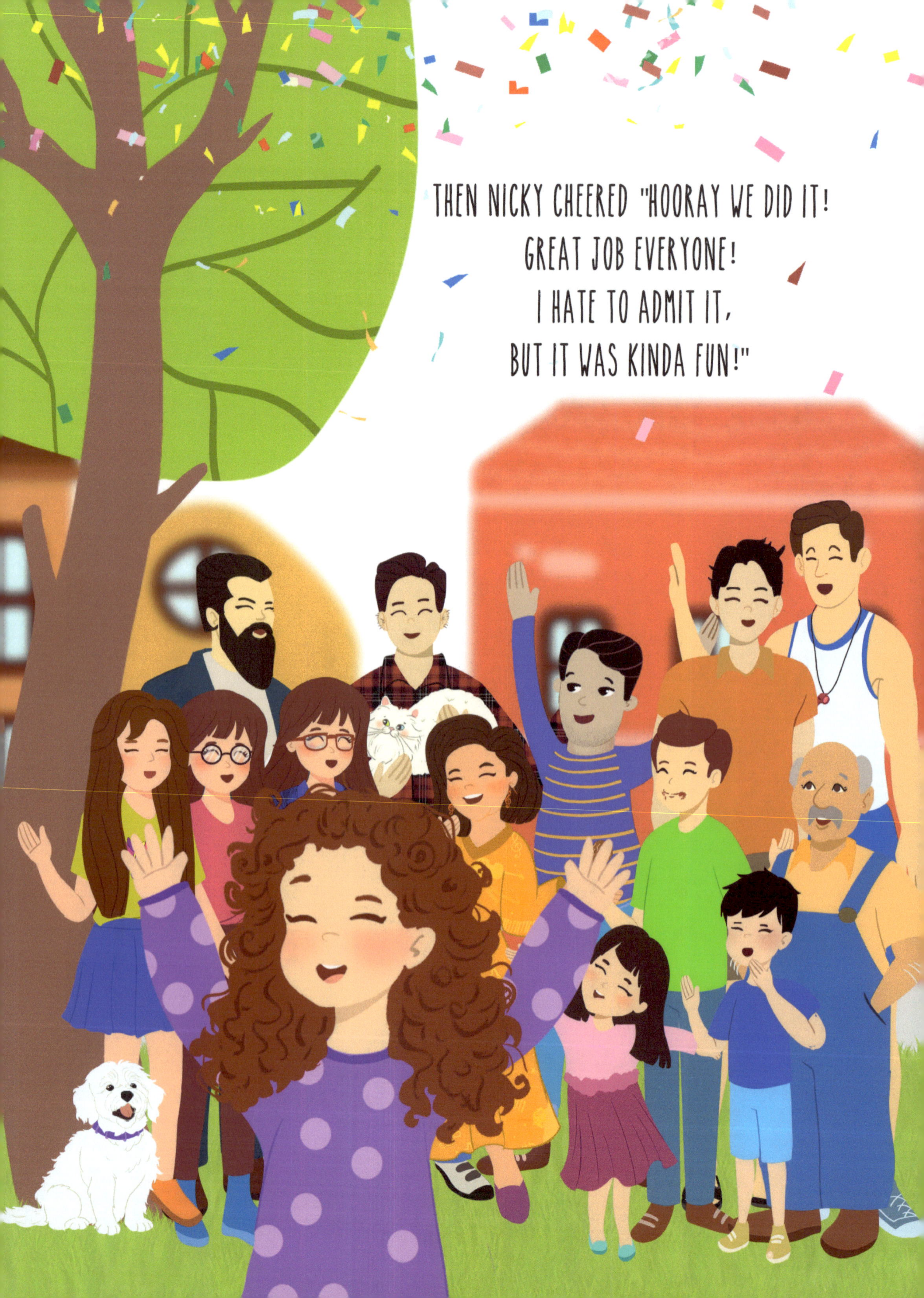
THEN NICKY CHEERED "HOORAY WE DID IT!
GREAT JOB EVERYONE!
I HATE TO ADMIT IT,
BUT IT WAS KINDA FUN!"

WHATEVER MADE JESSEE CLIMB THAT TREE?
WHATEVER MADE HER FILL WITH ANXIETY??

THEN NICKY SHOUTED, "JESSEE CLIMBED THAT TREE
BECAUSE IT'S THE 6TH DAY OF JUNE!
THAT'S 8 DAYS AWAY FROM THE STRAWBERRY MOON!!"

MOONS HAVE A WAY
OF GATHERING PEOPLE TOGETHER
NO MATTER HOW TALL OR SHORT
NO MATTER THE WEATHER
JUNE
M T W T F S S
1 2 3 4
5 6 7 8 9 10 11
12 13 14 15 16 17 18
19 20 21 22 23 24 25
26 27 28 29 30

SO IN THE NEXT 8 DAYS
JOIN US, YES YOU!
WOULDN'T YOU LOVE TO BE PART
OF THIS HUDSON STREET HULLABALOO??

JUNE 14
FULL MOON PARTY
EVERYONE MEET
334 HUDSON STREET!

CAN YOU
NAME THEM?

www.ingramcontent.com/pod-product-compliance
Lightning Source LLC
Chambersburg PA
CBHW041415300726
48978CB00002B/101